FRANKENSTEIN

TREASURY OF ILLUSTRATED CLASSICS™

FRANKENSTEIN

by
Mary Shelley

Adapted by
C. Louise March

Illustrated by
Bob Berry

Modern Publishing
A Division of Unisystems, Inc.
New York, New York 10022

Series UPC: 38150

Cover art by Bob Berry

Contents

CHAPTER 1

Robert Walton's Correspondence

To Mrs. Saville, England
St. Petersburg, December 11, 17–

Dear Sister,

You will be happy to hear that yesterday I arrived safely at my destination. I know that you are worried about my voyage and the dangers that I will face in order to succeed.

I am already far north of London. As I walk through the streets of St. Petersburg, the cold northern breeze seems to call me onward. It is just a hint of the icy climate that I must still travel

through. But at the Pole, which I will one day reach, the sun is forever visible.

What might be found in a country of eternal light? Perhaps there, my hunger for adventure will be satisfied. All of my fears of danger or death disappear when I see this vision before me. If I discover a passage near the Pole to those countries—which now take many months to reach—or unravel some secret of the magnet, then humanity will have benefited.

It has taken six years, but I am now realizing my dreams. To prepare my body for the extreme climate that I must pass though to reach the Pole, I accompanied the whale-fishers on several expeditions to the North Sea. I endured cold, hunger, thirst, and exhaustion. I devoted my nights to the studying of all of the branches of science that would aid my expedition.

And now, dear Margaret, do I not deserve to achieve greatness? I might have passed my life in ease and luxury, but I prefer glory to wealth. My courage is firm, but I often doubt that I will achieve my purpose.

This is the most favorable time to travel in Russia. The Russians' sleds fly quickly over the snow and are far more agreeable than the English stagecoaches. The cold is bearable if you are wrapped in heavy coats and fur.

In a few weeks I shall depart St. Petersburg for Archangel. There I will hire a ship and as many sailors as I think necessary. I do not intend to sail until June. If I succeed, many months, perhaps years, will pass before I am able to return to you. But if I fail, you will see me again very soon—or never. Farewell, my dear sister.

With love,
Robert Walton

To Mrs. Saville, England
Archangel, March 28, 17–

Dear Margaret,

The time passes slowly here in this land of frost and snow. I have hired a ship and sailors that I believe to be courageous and dependable. Still, I yearn for a real companion, someone who can share the joys and sorrows of my grand adventure. I am in need of someone to help guide me in this perilous journey.

For the first fourteen years of my life I ran wild and read nothing but our Uncle Thomas's books. Now I am twenty-eight,

and my lack of education shows. My romantic dreams of adventure need to be reined in. I look in vain among merchants and seamen, for their lives are driven by necessity.

The winter has been severe, but spring has come remarkably early. Perhaps I may sail even sooner than I expected. Now that my journey is about to begin, I feel a mixture of exhilaration and fear. Yes, there is a dreamer in me. It is true that I seek fame and glory. But I am also a hard worker and concerned for the safety of the crew. I cannot promise you that all will go well, but I have great hope of seeing you again. In the meantime, please continue to write me. Your letters bring me such comfort.

Your affectionate brother,
Robert Walton

To Mrs. Saville, England
August 5, 17–

Dearest Sister,
Although it is likely that you will see me before this letter reaches you, I must record the strange things that have taken place.

Last Monday we were almost completely surrounded by ice. It closed in on the ship on all sides, scarcely leaving her room to bob in the sea. Adding to the danger was a thick, blinding fog. At about two o'clock the mist cleared away, and we saw, stretched out in

every direction, vast and irregular
plains of ice. The crew grew anxious
and, I must admit, so did I.

The appearance of a sled drawn by
dogs, which passed northward half a
mile away, drew our minds away from
the danger. The figure who sat in the sled
and guided the dogs along the ice was
enormous. We viewed his rapid progress
through our telescopes. Since we were
shut in by ice, it was impossible to follow
his tracks. Before nightfall, the ice broke

and our ship was free.

In the morning, I went on deck and found the sailors talking to someone in the sea. I saw a sled like the one we had seen the night before. It had drifted toward us on a large fragment of ice.

Only one sled dog remained alive. A human being lay inside the carriage. The sailors were urging him to board our ship. He certainly was not the giant we had seen through our telescopes. When I came on deck one sailor said, "Here is *our captain, and he will not allow you to die on the open sea."*

The stranger spoke to me in English, but he had a foreign accent. "Before I come on board your vessel," he said, "will you tell me where you are headed?"

Astonished that he did not gladly scramble on board, I replied that we sought the Northern Pole. When he heard this, he nodded his head, and the men helped him on board. His body was still, lean, and frozen. Before we could carry him into the cabin, he fainted. We worked to revive him on the deck. As soon as he began to move again, we

wrapped him up in blankets and placed him near the chimney of the kitchen stove. Slowly, he recovered and ate some hot soup, which restored him.

Two days passed before he was able to speak again. Then I had him taken to my own cabin, and I cared for him when I could. His looks are quite remarkable. His eyes are wild—even mad—but if anyone is kind to him, his face lights up. Generally, he is depressed. It is clear that his mind is weighted down with a great burden.

I tried to restrain the sailors from distressing him further by asking questions, but the lieutenant asked why he had come so far upon the ice in his sled.

"To follow a bitter enemy," he replied.

"Does this man travel in a sled?" the lieutenant asked.

"Yes," he said.

"Then we have seen him," the lieutenant replied. "The day before we rescued you we saw a sled across the ice.

Aboard it was a man of monstrous proportions."

The stranger became very agitated when he heard this. He tried to discover which direction the demon, as he called him, traveled.

Later, the stranger asked me if I thought that the other sled had been destroyed when the ice broke. I replied that the traveler might have arrived at a place of safety before the ice broke, but I could not be certain. After this exchange, I noticed that he became more animated. He was eager to be on deck to watch for the other sled. By promising that someone else would keep watch, I persuaded

him to rest in the cabin.

The stranger has gradually improved in health but is very silent and appears uneasy when anyone except me enters his cabin. I must tell you that I have taken to him like a brother. I am troubled by his grief and despair. He must have been a noble man in his better days. I said in one of my letters that I thought I would never find a friend on the wide ocean. I believe that I have found such a man who, before his spirit was broken by misery, would have been a true companion.

R. W.

To Mrs. Saville, England
August 13, 17–

Dear Margaret,

My affection for my guest increases every day. He is gentle and wise. Much recovered from his illness, he is always on deck watching for his "demon" on the sled.

One day, as I spoke to my new friend, he became gloomy. He placed his hands over his eyes, and I saw tears trickle between his fingers. He exclaimed, "Let me reveal my tale!"

With these words, he collapsed, and many hours of rest were necessary to restore his composure. He turned his attention upon me, asking for the history of my earlier years. I spoke of my desire for a friend and expressed my belief that a man could boast of little happiness if he did not have such a friend.

He heartily agreed with me and said, "I once had for a friend the most noble of human creatures. I have lost him, and far more than he. You have hope, and the world before you, and have no cause for despair. But I have lost everything and cannot begin life anew."

R. W.

To Mrs. Saville, England
August 19, 17—

Dear Margaret,
  Yesterday the stranger said to me, "You seek knowledge and wisdom, as I once did. I hope that your desires may not be a serpent to sting you, as mine have been.
  "I had hoped that my story would die with me, yet when I think that you may be on the same course, exposing yourself to the same dangers that have destroyed me, I am driven to share this tale with you."

R. W.

Here is the story of how Victor Frankenstein became the haunted figure that Robert Walton saved from drowning in the frigid seas. Told to and recorded by Walton, these words reproduce as nearly as possible those of Frankenstein himself.

CHAPTER 2

The Frankenstein Family History

My place of birth is Geneva, Switzerland. My ancestors have held many public offices and were trusted public servants. My father continued to follow in this lineage and was known for his loyalty and honor. His dedication to his career delayed his marriage until later in life.

A dear friend of my father's was a merchant named Beaufort. He fell upon hard times. After paying his debts, Beaufort left Geneva and his past, settling with his daughter, Caroline, in the town of Lucerne.

My father loved Beaufort and was deeply grieved by his friend's circumstances. So he offered to provide the means for his friend to reestablish himself. After searching for nearly a year, he discovered Beaufort's house. Beaufort had saved only a very small sum of money from the wreck of his fortunes, but it was sufficient to provide for him and his daughter for some months. He hoped to find employment in a merchant's house, but while he was idle his misfortune played upon his mind and drew all of the strength from

his body. His daughter cared for his every need, but she saw that their money would soon run out. Caroline was strong and courageous, and she found some work to provide a meager subsistence.

Despite Caroline's valiant efforts, Beaufort grew worse. She was forced to spend more time caring for him, leaving little time to work.

Before long, he died, and she was left alone. Just then, my father entered the house. He took Caroline back to Geneva and put her in the care of a relative. Although he was much older than she was, two years later they married. They cherished each other, and my father took great care to attend to all of her needs and wishes.

Since her health had suffered during her father's exile, my father thought that the pleasant climate of Italy and the change of scene would restore her. From Italy they visited Germany and

France. I was born in Naples, and as an infant accompanied them in their travels. For several years I had them all to myself, and they showered me with devotion, love, and lessons of patience, charity, and discipline.

When I was five years old, we spent a week near Lake Como. While there, my parents often visited the cottages of the peasants and attended to many of their needs.

One day, when my father had gone by himself to Milan, my mother and I visited a poor family with five hungry children. One of the children stood out. She had golden hair, blue eyes and the sweetest face. Her parents had died, leaving her a penniless orphan. This girl captured my parents' hearts. With the peasant family's blessings, they adopted the girl. This lovely child, named Elizabeth Lavenza, became my constant childhood companion.

CHAPTER 3

The Golden Age of Childhood

Elizabeth and I were not quite a year apart in age, but our personalities and desires were very different. She was calm and patient. I was eager and impatient. While I immersed myself in the world of science, Elizabeth was drawn to the beauties of nature and poetry. She delighted in the things themselves, and I wanted to pick them apart and understand how they worked.

When I turned seven, my mother had another child and later another. These were Ernest and William. At that

time, my parents chose to stay close to Switzerland, their native country, and stop their wandering through Europe.

We had a home in Geneva but lived most of the year in a house on the eastern shore of Lake Belrive. My close tie with Elizabeth and my natural bent for seclusion kept me isolated from most of my school fellows. I did find one true friend in Henry Clerval, the son of a Genevese merchant. Henry longed to follow in the footsteps of the medieval knights of old. With the

friendship of Elizabeth and Henry and the wise and loving protection of my parents, I had a wonderful childhood.

When I was thirteen we visited Thonon. One day, bad weather confined us to the inn. In the library, I came upon the works of Cornelius Agrippa, an alchemist. His theories were very exciting and interesting to me. But when I showed the books to my father, he said, "My dear Victor, do not waste your time. It is all fantasy." But I continued to read with great attention. When I returned home, I acquired all of Agrippa's available works and those led me to Paracelsus and Albertus Magnus. I studied the wild fancies of these writers with delight.

My opinion of the giants of modern science sunk and I took these alchemists' word as truth. Wealth meant nothing to me, but I began to dream of the fame I would receive if I

could banish disease and discover the source of health and life. The ancient philosophers promised that death was not the inevitable end of life and that those who had died could be raised again.

When I was about fifteen, we witnessed a most violent and terrible thunderstorm while at our house on Belrive. I watched as it advanced from behind the mountains. As I stood at the door, I saw a stream of fire pierce an old oak, which stood about twenty yards from our house. When the dazzling light vanished, the oak had disappeared and nothing remained but a blasted stump.

When we went the next morning for a closer look, we found the tree had shattered in a remarkable manner: It was not splintered by the shock, but entirely reduced to thin ribbons of wood.

It was our luck to have with us a man of great learning in the field of natural philosophy. He began to enthusiastically discuss his theory of electricity. He believed that shocks of electricity could actually bring an inanimate thing to life. What he said cast all thoughts of Cornelius Agrippa out of my mind. I turned my attention to mathematics and the modern sciences. I believe that had I continued in this direction, the course of my life would have been much different. I would have been saved from the horrors of subsequent years. But this was not to be.

CHAPTER 4

Victor Leaves Home

When I was seventeen, my parents sent me to Germany to go to college. As the day I was to leave grew closer, the first tragedy in my sad tale occurred. Elizabeth was stricken with scarlet fever. Although we urged my mother not to care for Elizabeth herself, she would not hear of it. Elizabeth was brought back to life through my dear mother's loving care, but at the expense of my mother's life. Unlike Elizabeth, my mother's condition did not improve.

On her deathbed she expressed her

wishes for Elizabeth and me. "My children," she said, "my firmest hopes of future happiness were placed on the prospect of your marriage. Your union will console your father. Elizabeth, my love, you must take my place and look after the younger children. My life has been happy and full. I rejoice to know that you are together, and that you will be with me again."

My mother was dead, and we grieved heavily. Although I looked forward to my studies, I delayed my departure. Elizabeth was our angel. Despite her own grief, she devoted herself to reviving our spirits and preserving the memory of Mother in her smiles and gestures.

Finally the day of my departure for college arrived. Henry spent the last evening with us. On this last evening, my dear friend was sad.

With great reluctance we finally said our farewells and went to bed. At dawn,

I walked down to the carriage. To my surprise, my father, Elizabeth, and Henry were waiting to wish me well.

After a long and tiring journey, I saw the high, white steeple of Ingolstadt. I spent that first night in this new town by myself, in my solitary apartment.

The next morning I wasted no time in introducing myself to the university's foremost professors. As fate would have it, my first meeting was with Professor Krempe, who taught natural philosophy.

Professor Krempe was a coarse man, but at the top of his field. When he asked about my interests, I casually

mentioned the alchemists I had formerly regarded so highly.

"Have you really spent your time studying such nonsense?" he asked, astonished.

When I nodded, he continued, "Every minute that you have wasted on those books is entirely lost. I never expected in this age to find a disciple of Albertus Magnus. My dear sir, you must begin your studies all over again."

He wrote down a list of several books that he wanted me read and gave me his lecture schedule. He mentioned that a Professor Waldman would lecture on chemistry on the alternate days. Then I was dis-

missed.

Although I had thought better of my fascination with the great alchemists, I still disdained modern natural philosophy. It was very different in those long ago days when the masters of science had looked for power and immortality. Such views, although futile, were grand. But now, the ambition of the natural philosophers seemed limited to disproving those visions on which my interest in science was chiefly founded. They wanted me to exchange grand dreams for realities of little worth.

During the next few days, I considered all of this as I worked to acquaint myself with the university and the way of life here.

The following week, lectures began, but I could not bring myself to listen to Professor Krempe. In my judgment, he was rude and conceited. I remembered that Professor Waldman would be lecturing on alternate days. I decided to go hear what he had to say.

Professor Waldman was about fifty years of age, and quite different from Professor Krempe. His face was open and kind. He was short, but since he stood very straight, he gave the impression of great stature and dignity. His voice was very sweet.

His lecture began with an overview of the history of chemistry and the major achievements made by various researchers. Next he discussed the present state of science and explained its basic concepts. He finished with an unforgettable ode to the possibilities of modern science.

"The ancient teachers of chemistry," he began, "promised impossibilities and performed almost nothing. The modern masters, on the other hand, promise very little. They know that what the ancients sought—immortality—is but a dream. But modern-day philosophers have performed miracles. They have

discovered some of nature's deepest secrets. Among their revelations are the system by which blood circulates and the nature of the air we breathe. They have acquired new and almost unlimited powers."

I cannot express how these words shook up my understanding. So much has been done, I thought. More, far more, will be achieved. Following in these footsteps, I will pioneer a new way, explore unknown powers, and unfold to the world the deepest mysteries of creation.

That night, Professor Waldman's words echoed through my brain. I firmly resolved to devote myself to a science for which I believed I was fit. The next day I paid Professor Waldman a visit. He welcomed me and listened with great kindness to my account of how I hoped to contribute to the advances of modern science.

Whereas Professor Krempe had mocked me, Professor Waldman said, "The work of men of genius, however wrongly directed, hardly ever fails to open the eyes of men to new possibilities." I wholeheartedly agreed. I told him that his lecture had removed my prejudices against modern chemists.

CHAPTER 5

Victor Dreams of Glory

From that day forward, my studies became everything to me. In Professor Waldman I found a true friend. His gentleness, instruction and honesty sweetened the difficult life I had chosen for myself. My labors were well rewarded, and soon I was considered a talented pupil.

Two years passed in which I thought of nothing but my studies. Consumed by my desire to find something that had never been unearthed by my forerunners, I thought little of my loved ones back home. The success of my research drew the attention of the professors and my fellow students.

When I had arrived at this point, I realized that my professors had taught me all that they could. I thought of returning to Geneva. But as fate would have it, an incident kept me at Ingolstadt.

During the course of my work at the university, I came to ask myself about the source of life. Other students had looked into curing disease and prolonging life. But fear and superstition had kept many from a closer examination of life's beginnings.

I then turned my attention to the study of the human body. It seemed logical to me that in order to examine the causes of life, one must first look at death. Thus, in addition to anatomy, I also observed natural decay in the human body. In churchyards, I found materials to examine.

If I had not been taken over by a thirst for glory, I believe that I would not have had the strength for the horrors of this

task. And the reward for this sinister work was no less than to give life to lifeless matter. You may call me a madman, but I succeeded where no other man had.

I will not lead you on the same journey of destruction that I have traveled. For you see, I was not content with creating a being of simpler organization. I set my sights on giving life to another being like myself—a man. It was with these feelings that I began the creation of a human being. The minuteness of the parts with which I worked slowed my progress, so I decided that this being should be about eight feet in height, with a similar body of massive proportions.

In time, I grew pale, thin and worn. My work experienced high points and very low points when I thought I had utterly failed. I walked the streets, a gaunt, half-crazed figure. I toiled endlessly into the night. In a solitary chamber at the top of the house, I kept the hideous materials that I found in the graves, dissecting room and slaughterhouse. The summer months passed unnoticed. I did not correspond with my family, and I knew that my silence must have alarmed them.

By the end of fall, I could see that I was succeeding in my task. Every night I was oppressed by a slow fever. I became nervous to a most painful degree. Even the fall of a leaf startled me. I shunned my fellow creatures as if I were guilty of a crime. My appearance was, indeed, frightening. But I reassured myself that once my task was accomplished, I could again enjoy the pleasures and pastimes of a normal life.

CHAPTER 6

Frankenstein Creates a Monster

It was on a dreary November evening that I beheld the results of the past months' madness. It was one o'clock in the morning. The rain pattered dismally against the panes. My candle was nearly burned out when, by the glimmer of the half-extinguished light, I saw the dull yellow eye of the creature open. It breathed hard, and a convulsive motion agitated its limbs.

I had hoped to create a man of great beauty. Yet this creature's sallow skin stretched uncomfortably over its jaws and cheekbones. His long black hair and pearly white teeth only served to

highlight his fiendish features. I became sickened when I looked into his watery eyes, and I fled the room. I paced the floor of my bedroom, unable to stop the whirl of judgments spinning through my mind.

Finally, I threw myself onto the bed and fell into a deep and troubled sleep. After a bad dream, I bolted up from the bed. The light of the moon came dimly through the window and framed the miserable monster I had created. He held up the curtain of the bed, his eyes fixed on me. His jaw opened, and he muttered some sounds while a grin wrinkled his cheeks. In terror, I raised myself and, though he put out an arm as if to detain me, I escaped and rushed downstairs. I took refuge in the courtyard and stayed there the rest of the night.

Finally morning dawned, dismal and wet. I would not dare return to my apartment. I hurried through the streets drenched with rain but eager to

avoid the monster, which I feared watched my every move.

Coming to an inn, I noticed a coach traveling toward me. It stopped, and my dear friend Henry Clerval sprang out. Shocked, I thought this was also part of my nightmare. When I realized that it was, indeed, Henry, my mind was flooded with questions about my father, Elizabeth, and Geneva. We walked toward the university as Henry filled me in on events back home.

As we neared the university, I began to fear that the monster was still in my apartment. I told my friend to wait at the bottom of the stairs. A cold shiver came over me when I opened the door, but there was no monster. I clapped my hands for joy and ran down to Henry. The servant brought breakfast, and we settled down to eat.

But Clerval took note of my odd behavior. "My dear Victor," he said, "what is the matter? How ill you are!"

"Do not ask me!" I cried. I covered my eyes with my hands, for I thought I saw the monster glide into the room. "*He* can tell you!" I screamed. "Oh, save me!" I struggled and fell down in a fit. I did not regain consciousness for quite some time.

Slowly, and with frequent relapses that alarmed my friend, I recovered. It was now springtime. When I was able, I thanked Henry and asked how I could repay his kindness in caring for me. He pushed aside the thought, but indicated that he would very much like to know what had contributed to my sickness. When he saw my face cloud over once again, he assured me that he would drop the subject.

Then he handed me a letter he had just received from my dear Elizabeth, and the shadow lifted.

CHAPTER 7

Letters from Home

To Mr. Frankenstein, Ingolstadt
Geneva, March 18, 17–

Dear Victor,

You have been very ill. The constant letters from dear Henry do not reassure me enough. For a long time I have thought that each post would bring us good news in your own handwriting. Henry writes that you are getting better. I hope that you will confirm this soon yourself.

Get well and return to us. You will find a happy, cheerful home and friends who dearly love you. Your father's

health is good, and you would be pleased to see your brother, Ernest! He is now sixteen and full of spirit. I also wish you could see your youngest brother, William. He is tall for his age, with sweet blue eyes and curly hair. He is a favorite with the ladies.

Since you left us, only one change has taken place in our little household. Do you remember how Justine Moritz came to our family? Her mother was a widow with four children, of whom Justine was the third. This girl had always been the favorite of her father, but her mother treated her badly. After the father died,

Justine's life became very hard. Your mother, aware of the situation, asked Justine's mother to part with the twelve-year-old girl, who came to live with us as a cherished family friend and servant.

Justine was well educated and extremely grateful to your mother and the family. When your mother was ill, Justine tenderly nursed her, and she suffered when your mother died.

Then, one by one, Justine's siblings died, and her mother was left with no one to care for her. Putting aside the past, Justine went home to care for her mother. Well, her mother died, and now Justine has returned to us.

Write, dearest Victor! We are deeply grateful to Henry for his kindness, his affection and his many letters.

Take care of yourself!

Elizabeth

I thought of the many hours that I

had spent with Elizabeth, and of her gentle, loving ways. I immediately wrote back to her. After a few more weeks of rest I was able to leave my apartment. I introduced Henry to several professors. He was very eager to begin his studies. Although restored to health, I had lost my interest in my work.

I intended to return to Geneva at the end of autumn. Several circumstances delayed my departure, and then winter came on with a fury. Snow fell heavily, and the roads were impassable. Spring came late, but by May I expected to soon begin the journey home.

Henry proposed a tour of Ingolstadt and the surrounding countryside as a fitting close to my time here. We spent a few weeks in this way, and my strength and spirits greatly improved. We returned to the university on a Sunday afternoon. The fine weather had everyone in good cheer and, at least for the present, the dread that had surrounded me prior to our trip was far from my mind.

This peace was brief, for when I entered my apartment there was a letter from my father waiting for me.

To Frankenstein, Ingolstadt
Geneva, May 12, 17—

My dear Victor,
This letter, which would have brought good tidings and a date upon which you would return to us, is the bearer of bitter news. How, Victor, can I start to tell you of our misfortune? Our William, our sweet child, is dead! Last Thursday, I went with Elizabeth, Ernest and William

for a walk. At dusk, when we turned toward home, we found that William and Ernest, who had traveled ahead, were no longer with us. We took a seat and waited, thinking that they would soon return. When Ernest came, he asked if we had seen William. In their play, William had run off. Ernest expected him to come back, but he never did. We calmed ourselves by saying that William must surely have gone home to wait for us.

But when we arrived there, no one had seen William. We set out with torches to search, and at about five in the morning I found my dear boy stretched motionless on the grass, red lines on his neck indicating how the murderer had achieved his evil ends.

We had left Elizabeth back home in case William returned there. When she heard what had happened, she insisted on seeing his body. When we showed it to her, she claimed that she had mur-

dered William! She collapsed from the strain of the news, but later she told me how that same evening William had asked her to let him wear a very valuable locket which held a picture of your mother. This picture is now gone. It appears to be the motive for the murder.

We are grateful that your mother is not alive to have to bear this. We need you, Victor. Your presence will console us. Please come home as soon as you can.

Your affectionate father,
Alphonse Frankenstein

Henry watched my face as I read. I handed the letter to him and turned away so he couldn't see the tears that were streaming down my face. After reading the letter, Henry's eyes filled with tears too. He asked me what I was going to do.

"I am going to travel home to Geneva. Come with me to order the horses," I said.

CHAPTER 8

Who Murdered William?

I left Henry in Ingolstadt and began the saddest journey I had yet taken. My urgency to reach my family lessened as I came closer to Geneva. I dreaded seeing their faces. I decided to stay two days in Lausanne, giving myself time to gather my strength.

It was dark when Geneva came into view. The gates of the town were already shut, forcing me to spend the night in a village about a mile from the city. Since I could not sleep, I decided to visit the murder site. Although I could not pass

through the town, I found a boat to carry me to the place.

As I crossed the water, lightning played on the summit of Mont Blanc. When I landed, the storm broke and rain fell from the sky in large drops.

A flash of light shot through the trees, framing a figure. It was the monster! And at that moment, I knew who had murdered my brother. Enraged, I tried to pursue him but, with another flash of light, he was gone. Nearly two years had passed since I had created this being. Was this his first crime? I spent the rest of the night cold and wet, but my mind was so absorbed in my misery that I barely noticed.

I woke at dawn and walked toward town. I hoped to make known the true story of William's death, but when I played it over in my head I knew it would sound like the ravings of a madman.

It was about five in the morning

when I entered my father's house. I told the servants not to disturb the family, and went into the library to wait. I thought about the six years that had passed since I'd last stood here. I looked at the picture of my mother, which hung over the mantel. Below this portrait was one of William. I broke down in tears.

Soon, Ernest came in. His own tears joined mine and, as they did so, the full weight of our loss came upon me. I asked Ernest about Elizabeth.

"She, most of all," said Ernest, "needs your strength and consolation. She accused herself of having caused William's death, but since the murderer has been discovered—"

"The murderer discovered!" I shouted. "How can that be? It is impossible. I saw him. He was free last night!"

"I do not understand you, Victor. The murderer is not a 'he.' When you hear the name of the accused, it will add to your misery. No one would believe it at first.

But now only Elizabeth remains uncon- vinced. It is Justine Moritz!" Ernest said.

"Justine Moritz?" I asked.

Ernest gave me as much informa- tion as he could. On the morning fol- lowing the murder, Justine had been found ill and was confined to her bed for several days afterward. During this time, one of the servants found in her pocket the picture of my mother, which seems to have been the motive for the crime.

"You are all mistaken," I assured my brother. "I know the true identity of the murderer. Justine is innocent."

At that moment my father came into the room. Although deeply distressed, he tried to be cheerful. But Ernest exclaimed, "Papa! Victor says that he knows who murdered William."

"We do also," my father replied, sadly shaking his head. "I would rather have been forever ignorant than to learn of Justine's betrayal."

"My dear father, you are mistaken.

Justine is innocent!" I said.

Soon Elizabeth joined us. I noted that since I saw her last, she had changed. She was no longer a child. She welcomed me with the greatest affection. "Your arrival," she said, "fills me with hope. Perhaps you will find some way to prove Justine's innocence. Now, our misfortune is doubly hard on us. We have not only lost our darling boy, but this poor girl, whom I sincerely love, is to be torn away by an even worse fate. If she is condemned, I will never again be truly happy."

"She is innocent," I said firmly. "That shall be proved."

CHAPTER 9

Justine's Trial

Justine's trial was set for eleven o'clock. We still had a few hours to pass before the grim event. The shock and horror of the situation had stunned us all. Not only was poor, innocent William lost, but now Justine was to die and her reputation forever ruined by her conviction as a murderess!

When we entered the courtroom, I saw that Justine was calm. She wore mourning clothes. When she entered the court, her eyes slowly scanned the audience and settled upon our family. Tears came to her eyes, but she brushed them away and composed herself.

After the prosecutor stated the charge, several witnesses were called, and the incriminating facts were recounted.

Justine had been out the entire night upon which William had been murdered. Toward morning, a woman heading to the market saw Justine at the very spot where William was later found. When the woman asked Justine why she was out so early, Justine mumbled and seemed confused. Justine returned to the house about eight o'clock. Another servant asked her where she had passed the night. Justine answered that she had been looking for William and demanded earnestly if anything had been heard concerning him. When shown the body, she became hysterical and lay agitated in bed for several days.

There was a pause and then the only evidence—my mother's locket—

was produced. Elizabeth, her voice quivering, confirmed that it was the same locket that she had given William an hour before his disappearance. Sounds of disgust filled the court.

Then Justine spoke in her own defense. "I am innocent of this evil crime," she said. "I will not trouble the court with my protests, but will rely on a plain and simple explanation of the facts."

Justine said that, with Elizabeth's permission, she had spent the evening of that night at the house of her aunt in Chene, a village about a mile from Geneva. She returned to Geneva about nine o'clock and met a man who asked her if she had seen William. His absence alarmed her, and she spent the next few hours looking for the child. Forgetting the passage of time in her haste to find William, Justine was locked out of the city when the gates were closed for the night. Finding a barn near a cottage, she went in for a few hours of shelter. Since she knew the cottage dwellers fairly well, she did not think to wake them up and ask their permission. When dawn came, she rose to continue her search. When the market woman questioned her, she could not speak clearly, for worry and exhaustion clouded her mind.

She did not have an explanation for the locket that was found in her clothing. She was unaware of anyone who wished her ill. It seemed odd that someone would commit a murder to obtain a jewel, only to leave it behind.

Then, she asked that a few witnesses be called to testify for her good character. Many who could have given such testimony spoke well of her, but fear and horror of the crime left them nervous and reserved. The truth is that most people thought Justine was guilty! Seeing this, Elizabeth came forward to speak, quite passionately, on Justine's behalf.

Certainly, Elizabeth's eloquent and heartfelt testimony drew approval from the audience. But their knowing glances and nods were directed in sympathy for Elizabeth and our family's goodness toward Justine. This further increased their rage that an ungrateful servant could commit this atrocity. I reserved my pity for myself, for having created the monster that had caused the deaths of my brother, and now Justine.

After a night of tossing and turning sleeplessly in my bed, I went to the court to find out the verdict. Justine

had been condemned to death as a murderess.

Justine asked to see Elizabeth before being executed. I went with Elizabeth to visit Justine one last time. We entered the gloomy prison chamber and saw Justine sitting on some straw at the far end. Justine asked me if I believed her to be guilty. Elizabeth told her that I was even more convinced now of Justine's innocence. Justine thanked me and said that my kindness added to her peace. We said our good-byes and left.

The next day, Justine was executed. I now had the deaths of William and Justine on my conscience, as well as the misery of my whole family.

CHAPTER 10

The Monster Finds Victor

In need of a change of scenery and peaceful surroundings, my family and I went to our house at Belrive. The gates to the city were locked each night, so the chance to roam freely around the lake at night lifted my spirits a bit. Often, after the rest of the family had retired for the night, I took the boat out. Sometimes, with my sails set, I was carried by the wind.

At other times, after rowing into the middle of the lake, I left the boat to follow its own course while I thought over the recent past. Justine's conviction, in particular, was troubling. Elizabeth still believed in Justine's innocence, but I was the only one who was certain of it. I wondered where the monster was and what he would do next. I was convinced that he was planning more evil deeds, and I was determined to prevent them.

Although Elizabeth did her best to console me, I slipped further into utter despair. Nonetheless, the change of place and my outdoor activities occasionally provided some relief.

One day I felt an urge to travel toward the Alpine valleys. My wanderings led me to the valley of Chamounix. I had visited it frequently during my childhood. A long time had passed since then, and it was hard to recall those carefree, happy days.

I began my journey on horseback. It was the middle of August—two months after Justine's execution—and the weather was glorious. The huge mountains and precipices on every side, the sound of the river raging among the

rocks and the dashing of the waterfalls took my mind off my own despair. Ruined castles hanging on the cliffs and cottages dotting the landscape here formed a scene of great beauty. The mighty Alps and their white and shining pyramids and domes towered above all. Here, I could convince myself that everything that had passed was but a dream.

As I entered the valley of Chamounix, I saw no more ruined castles and fertile fields. In the evening, as I rested in an inn, the murmuring sounds coming from the valley lulled me into a peaceful sleep.

Next, I sought to conquer the summit of Montanvert. I decided to go without a guide, for I knew the path well enough, and I needed to be alone.

The landscape was desolate and severe, with steep rises and short windings. Trees lay broken and strewn on the ground, some entirely destroyed,

others bent, leaning upon the jutting rocks of the mountain or across other trees. Higher up, the path was crossed by ravines of snow, where stones continually rolled from above. As I traveled, rain poured from the dark sky and increased my sadness.

It was nearly noon when I reached the top of the mountain peak. I sat for some time and looked out over the sea of ice below.

Then the figure of a monstrous man,

some distance away, drew my eye, and I saw that he was running at an incredible pace. Where I had picked my way through the dangerous passages, he was bounding like a gazelle. Before I knew it, the massive creature—the monster I had created—stood in front of me. I could not control my rage, and screamed at him. "I will trample you to dust!" I cried. "If only, by killing you, I could restore the lives of those you have murdered!"

"Ah, it is true. All men hate those

who are outcasts," the monster said. "I want only for companionship and the understanding of my creator, yet even you despise me. I ask for one thing only: Do your duty to me and make for me a creature who will not hate me and who will be my comfort in isolation."

I refused to listen to his arguments, but he pleaded, "Listen to me, Frankenstein. You accuse me of murder, and yet you would, with a satisfied conscience, put an end to me. All I ask is that you listen to me. If, then, you still wish to destroy me, try your best."

When I protested, he said that his tale was long and the temperature was much too cold to remain out on the ice.

He started to lead me across the ice. In shock, I followed him to a hut. Unsure about how much I did, indeed, owe him, and curious about the details of William's murder, I consented.

CHAPTER 11

The Monster's Tale

He began his story by describing the painful and confused sensations of his body upon coming to life. After so many years of study, I could not help but be fascinated by these details. Having told of his painful adjustment to light, heat, hunger and thirst, his narrative took a different turn.

"I left your apartment and found a place to rest by the side of a brook," the monster said. "I drank from the brook, and then, lying down, fell asleep. It was dark when I awoke. Before I left your room I had taken some clothing to cover myself, but I still felt cold. After many days passed, I began to distinguish the many new sensations, and take in my surroundings to a fuller degree. When I tried to imitate the lovely sounds of the animals and birds, I only heard a harsh, grating sound. It frightened me.

"Food quickly became scarce, so I decided to find a place where it was in good supply. Wrapping myself up in my cloak, I struck across the woods toward the setting sun.

"Three days passed as I wandered through the woodlands and finally reached the open country. A great fall of snow had taken place the night before, and the fields were covered in a white blanket. My feet were frozen through, and walking caused me pain. I entered a small hut nearby and saw an old man preparing breakfast over a fire. When he turned and saw me, he shrieked and ran out of the hut. I saw an opportunity in this hut, which was warm and dry and contained food. I ate the bread and cheese left by the man and soon after fell asleep.

"The sun shone overhead when I awoke. I packed the remains of my breakfast and headed across the fields. By sunset I had arrived at a village. I was captivated by the charming arrangement of huts, cottages and stately houses.

"I entered one of the cottages. When I did so, the children there cried out and fled. Soon the whole village was

alive with cries. I was now the object of a violent attack and lost no time in escaping to the open country.

"When I was a good distance from the village, I found a hovel, attached to a poor cottage, and entered into it. My place of refuge was constructed of wood, but so low that I had difficulty sitting upright in it. The floor was the earth below my feet, and wind swept in through the many holes in the walls. Still, it was dry and away from my enemies.

"The next morning, I examined the situation. Looking out, I saw a man and cowered inside the hut. I felt it was dangerous to make my presence known. I ate my breakfast and was about to get a little water when I heard a step. Through a small hole in the wall I saw a young woman with a pail on her head. Her clothing was faded and worn, but clean. I was moved by her kind and gentle face, for its expression was one of deep sadness. She

walked out of sight, but soon returned carrying a pail filled with milk. A young man met her. His expression held even greater pain than the woman's. I wondered what had caused these people to be so downhearted. Had they experienced the same betrayal of man now known to me in my wretchedness?

"I found that the wall of my hovel contained a boarded-up window, which opened into the cottage. There was a space in the boards that allowed me to see the cottage's interior. It was one

small room, whitewashed and clean but with little furniture. In one corner, near a small fire, sat an old man. The young woman finished her chores and then took something out of a drawer, put it in the old man's hands, and sat down beside him. He used the thing to make sweet sounds. The sound brought tears to the young woman's eyes.

"The sun began to set, and the young man appeared with wood for the fire. He and the young woman prepared their supper. The kindness with which they did all these things tore at my heart. As darkness covered the sky, the young woman lit candles. After that, I heard the young man begin to speak. I know now that he was reading aloud to the others. A short time later they blew out the candles and went to sleep. How I longed for a touch of kindness from these good people."

CHAPTER 12

The Lady on Horseback

"The family's daily occupations did not vary. Each day they applied themselves to their basic needs and few entertainments. I realized that the old man could not see. The man and woman devotedly attended to his every need. Their sadness troubled me. I wanted to know what had happened to them.

"Clearly, they were poor. At first I had helped myself to some of their food, but then I tried to add to it. I also replenished their wood, doing these things while they slept. These small gifts made them very happy and filled my heart with joy. I paid close attention to everything that happened in the cottage and even began repeating sounds and soon learning words. The young woman was called Agatha. The man's name was Felix, and his sadness outweighed the others' by far.

"My interest in these people was such that I felt I had to try to communicate with them. Perhaps if I could speak, they would not be so frightened of me. I could tell them my story and win their affection. My hopes were shattered when I took a look at myself in the pool of water. They, too, would despise me. But the old man was blind! Perhaps he would listen to my tale and plead my case to his companions.

"When the warmer weather arrived, the family was more active. They also had more food and seemed happier. Seeing them smile lifted my spirits, as well. It gave me courage to approach the old man.

"Before I could do so, the family

received a visit from a lady on horse-back and a man who served as her guide. Felix gave a shout of joy when he saw her. She wore a dark dress, and a thick black veil covered her face. She removed the veil and spoke in a lovely voice, but her language differed from that of the cottagers. Her beauty far sur-passed any I had seen in my travels.

"Felix turned to the old man and Agatha and told them about the woman. They smiled gently at her and took her hands. They communicated with her by signs. Hours passed in this way, and soon the stranger was trying to learn their language. Finally bedtime came, and Felix said good night to the woman. He called her Safie.

"In the morning, Felix and Agatha did their chores, as usual. Safie sat with the old man. The days passed. Their happiness increased, and so did my command of their language. The books from which Felix read also broadened my understanding of the world of men. It made me consider my own situation. Where did I fit in? What kind of man was I? I had no money and no friends. My strength was far

greater, but my looks were hideou
could be kind and gentle if give
chance, but would anyone give
chance? The pain caused by thes
questions was far worse than tha
which I endured from cold, hunger
and thirst.

"Thus troubled, but still wanting to
make friends with this family and the
beautiful stranger, I decided to wait
until I knew more about them. As time
passed, I found out the details of this
family's sorrow.

"The old man's name was De Lacey.
He was from a well-to-do and respected
family in France. Not long before I came
to the hut, the family had lived quite
comfortably in Paris. His son, Felix, had
served in the French military. Agatha
had spent her time in pursuits deemed
suitable for a lady.

"Safie's father was the cause of the
family's downfall. A Turkish merchant,
he had lived for years in Paris. For

some unexplained reason, the French government seized his property and confined him in a prison. He was tried and then condemned to death. Along with many in Paris, Felix was outraged by the injustice. He was so moved by the man's plight that he helped Safie's father escape.

"Although he rejected all offers of a reward, Felix had fallen in love with the merchant's daughter, whom he met when she had visited her father in prison. The merchant promised the young man Safie's hand in marriage, as long as Felix escorted them both out of France. Of course, Felix assured the merchant that he would take them both to a safe place and that no payment was required. Still, Felix hoped that Safie would come to love him in return.

"Felix was overjoyed when Safie seemed to return his affection. She sent him several letters thanking him

and expressing her admiration. She told Felix her own history and the many reasons why she feared for her future. Her mother was a Christian Arab, enslaved by the Turks. Safie's father, attracted by her mother's beauty, married her. With her mother's guidance, Safie developed a love of freedom that was seriously restricted in women of her father's culture. After her mother died, Safie was terrified of returning to the East. She hoped to marry a man of her mother's faith and wanted to live in the West.

"Felix secured passports in the name of his father, Agatha, and himself. He used these to help the merchant and Safie escape from France.

"Unknown to the good and trusting Felix, the merchant had no intentions of letting Safie marry him. Meanwhile, the government of France spared no pains in discovering how the merchant escaped. They imprisoned old De Lacey

and Agatha. When Felix heard the news, he decided to return home and help them.

"Felix's efforts to free his father and sister were unsuccessful. They were in prison for five months before the trial. They were condemned to exile from their homeland, and all of their wealth was confiscated. Thus I found them, poor and miserable, in a small cottage in Germany.

"When news of Felix's fate reached Leghorn, the dishonest merchant told his daughter to forget about him. But Safie was good and honest. Her father's betrayal disgusted her. A few days later, the merchant told Safie that the French government knew their whereabouts and he must flee. He had hired a ship that was set to sail in a few hours. He left a servant to watch over Safie until some of his possessions, which had been saved from the French, arrived at Leghorn. Together with these things, Safie and the servant would travel east.

"Not only did Safie love Felix, she felt she could never give up her freedom, nor her mother's religion. Looking

through some of her father's letters she learned the name of the village near which Felix and his family had settled. Taking some of her jewels and the money left by her father, she left Italy with an attendant and departed for Germany."

CHAPTER 13

A Bitter Rejection

"Safie's presence at the cottage lightened the family's burdens. I continued to hope that I, too, could be part of this happiness. But then I looked at my reflection in the pool and knew that my hopes were foolish. They would hate me, as everyone before had.

"Autumn passed, and the landscape began to turn bleak once again. I was unhappy and lonely. In my desperation, I gathered my courage to approach old De Lacey. My opportunity came one sunny day when Felix took the women on a long country walk. After they left,

the old man picked up his instrument to play. After a while, he became sad and put it down. I saw my chance. After a moment's hesitation, I proceeded to the front door.

"I knocked. 'Who is there?' the old man asked. 'Come in.'

"I entered. 'Pardon this intrusion,' I said. 'I am a traveler in need of a little rest. I would be very grateful if you would allow me to remain here for a few minutes before the fire.'

"'Enter,' De Lacey said. 'My children

are not home. As I am blind, I am afraid I shall find it difficult to find food for you.'

"'Do not trouble yourself, my kind host. I have food. It is warmth and rest that I need,' I said. 'I am now going to ask help from a family I deeply admire. But I fear their rejection.'

"'Do not despair,' he said, trying to comfort me. 'To be friendless is indeed to be unfortunate. But the hearts of men, when unprejudiced, are full of brotherly love. If these friends are good, they will listen to your pleas. Where do these friends live?'

"'Near this spot,' I told him.

"He asked me to tell him the details of my situation, for he might be able to help. I could not restrain my cry of joy.

"'How can I thank you?' I asked. 'You are the first person to show me any bit of kindness.'

"Then I heard the young people returning. I seized De Lacey's hand and cried out, 'Save and protect me! You

and your family are the friends whom I seek. Do not desert me!'

"At that instant the cottage door opened, and Felix, Safie, and Agatha entered. The women screamed, then Agatha fainted, and Felix came at me, attempting to protect the others. I fled to my hovel, tears streaming down my face.

"I stayed in the hut until night fell. Then, in a rage, I ran wild through the woods. I cursed you and I cursed the day on which my body knew life.

"Exhausted, I fell asleep on some leaves. When dawn came, I rose and heard men's voices. Felix had given the alarm and I was again in danger of attack. I hid in some thick bushes and tried to calm myself. Perhaps De Lacey would tell Felix what I had said. Maybe if I returned they would not reject me. My mind was clouded in a swirl of thoughts. Worn out, I fell into a fitful sleep.

"When I awoke, I felt hungry. I found some food and then walked toward the cottage. It was quiet and peaceful. No one was moving about, doing errands, or enjoying the pleasant sunshine. Felix

soon appeared, with another man.

"Felix said that he must take his family from this place. He said that their lives were in danger. And so he left and I saw no more of the family that I had come to love.

"It was then that I truly knew utter misery. I desired revenge on all those who had tormented and rejected me. I reserved my worst condemnations for you, Frankenstein. You created me, and you abandoned me. The pain was too great at that moment. I had to relieve it in some way. I lit a dry tree branch and fanned the flames. Using the branch, I set the cottage and hut on fire. I watched with glee as they burned to the ground.

"I remembered hearing you mention Geneva as your home. Geography had been the topic of many conversations in the cottage, and I had learned how to find a way there. My travels took considerable time. I suffered greatly

from hunger and bad weather. These trials increased my anger. I had one thought only: to find you and make you pay for my suffering."

CHAPTER 14

The Monster Goes to Geneva

"I made the journey and rejoiced when Geneva came into view one evening. I rested in the fields surrounding the city while trying to decide on my next course of action. My thoughts were interrupted by the approach of a beautiful child. It occurred to me that perhaps this little creature was unprejudiced and had lived too short a time to know fear. He might not run in horror from me. I took hold of him as he passed. But as soon as he looked at my face, he screamed and struggled violently.

"'Let me go! My papa is Alphonse

Frankenstein. He will punish you if you do not let me go!' the boy cried.

"'Frankenstein! You belong to my enemy. Ah, you shall be my first victim,' I said. Before I knew what had happened, the child lay still at my feet.

"Triumphantly, I looked down at him and saw something glittering on his chest. It was a portrait of a lovely woman. I ran wildly around until I saw a barn, which was empty. Inside, a woman was sleeping on some straw. She was young and held the bloom of life and the promise of happiness. I bent over her, and she stirred. The thought of her screaming and running away from me was unbearable. I put the child's locket in her pocket. If I must suffer, then she would, too. The locket would be found and she would be put to death as the child's murderess. Revenge would be mine!

"Hear me now, Victor Frankenstein. My deeds have repulsed you and caused your life to be bitter. More pain is your lot unless you create a being—a woman who is my equal—to be a comfort and joy when all others have forsaken me."

Listening to the last part of his story, I hung my head in despair. How could I let this being loose upon the world—and with a companion capable of doing the same evil deeds?

"I refuse," I replied. "As long as you walk the earth, there is one too many evildoers to terrorize men."

He said, "If you will do this, you will

never see either of us again. I will take my bride to the farthest end of the earth."

I replied, "I know you to be a fiend and a murderer. How do I know that you will be peaceful and contented?"

He looked sadly at me. "You owe this to me. Alone, I am a fiend. With love, I can be kind and gentle," he said.

Did I owe him at least a chance at some happiness? I hesitated. Then I said, "I will do as you ask. But only if you promise to leave Europe forever, and every other place where man can be found."

"I swear," he cried. "If you grant my wish, you will never see either of us again. I will leave you now. But I will be watching you. I will know when you have finished your work. Then I will come back to receive the companion of my dreams."

After he left, I wandered aimlessly. Night was far advanced when I was halfway back to Geneva. I wept bitterly.

It was well into the morning when I reached the village. I gathered my things at the inn and immediately left for Geneva. I was in quite a state when I walked through the door of our family home. My wild appearance alarmed everyone. They asked many questions, but I refused to answer. I went to my room, dreading the day I would start to fulfill my promise to the monster.

CHAPTER 15

Victor's Dilemma

Although I had much to do to pre-pare for my gruesome task, I could-n't find the courage to begin. It would take weeks to collect all of the necessary materials, and I still had more research to do. But my health had improved, and my mind was clear.

In such a state, my promise to the monster did not seem so urgent. There still were times when a deep gloom covered me, but then I kept to myself. I passed those days on the lake alone in a little boat, watching the clouds and listening to the rippling of the waves. It was after my return from one

of these rambles that my father called me aside.

He remarked on the change in my appearance and spirits. But he said that he was concerned by my reluctance to talk freely among the family. He asked me if my reluctance had to do with Elizabeth and if there was another to whom I had promised my affection. I was shocked by his speech. I assured him that I felt no pressure to fulfill an unspoken obligation that was understood since our childhood. I loved

Elizabeth even more now than I had back then.

Greatly relieved, he suggested an immediate union between us. To me the idea of marrying Elizabeth at this time was out of the question. My promise to the monster once again seemed urgent. I could not hope to give Elizabeth any happiness while the monster stalked me. And if I was to form another being, I knew I could not do it here. The strain I would be under would be too great.

I told my father that I wanted to travel to England prior to the wedding. He agreed to my request. He and Elizabeth secretly asked Henry to join me at Strasbourg and continue on with me to England. While this limited the amount of solitude I would have for my work, I welcomed Henry's companionship. I also promised myself that, once the work was done, I could marry Elizabeth. This, indeed, was a reason to move forward with my dismal task. I did not worry about the monster troubling the family in my absence, for I felt sure that he would follow me to England.

I left at the end of September. Two days after I arrived, Henry arrived. Our plan was to travel down the Rhine in a boat from Strasbourg to Rotterdam. From there we would take a ship to London.

On a clear morning near the end of December we first saw the white cliffs of Britain. And finally, the numerous steeples of London appeared.

CHAPTER 16

Two Friends Abroad

We decided to remain in London for several months. Henry's thirst for adventure and love of learning was ignited by the many opportunities this city had to offer. Had I not created the fiend that now haunted my dreams, I would have been equally excited by this city. Now, I only dreaded what I had come to do in this place.

Henry intended to visit India, and he believed that in England he could best prepare for the journey. He was very busy and often asked me to accompany him on his errands. As I was now collecting materials for the

monster's companion and I needed my solitude, I frequently turned down his invitations.

In February we received an invitation from a Scottish friend we had made in Geneva to visit him in Scotland. We accepted and planned to travel north the following month.

After spending a week in Edinburgh, we were on our way to Perth, where our Scottish friend met us. But I was in no mood to laugh and talk with strangers.

I told Henry that I wished to make the tour of Scotland alone and would meet him back here in about a month's time. He tried to talk me out of it but, seeing my determination, he wished me well.

I hoped to find a remote area where I could do my work. I firmly believed that the monster was following me and would find me when I had fulfilled my promise to him. I chose the most remote island of the Orkneys as my workplace. One of the island's three huts was unoccupied. The hut had two rooms—one I could use as my labora-

tory. But it needed many repairs. I hired some men to do the repairs and bought some furniture. Here, in this desolate and shabby place, I settled down to do my work.

One evening, as I sat in my laboratory, my thoughts were diverted to the monster's pleas for mercy and compassion. The sun had set, and the moon was just rising from the sea. Since I did not have enough light to continue my work, I let my mind consider more deeply the promise I had made. There was no guarantee that the monster could fulfill his side of the bargain. If he alone could do such evil things, what might two such beings accomplish?

My heart sank with this thought. Just at that moment, when I looked up, I saw his face, lit by the moon's glow, staring through my window. A ghastly grin wrinkled his lips. Enraged, I tore my handiwork to pieces. When he saw me destroy his future mate, he screamed and ran away in a wild frenzy.

At that moment, I vowed never to comply with his wishes.

Several hours passed in which I gazed at the sea. The shock and horror of seeing the monster's face had filled me with despair. At some point during the night, I heard the paddling of oars. Someone had landed a boat on the shore and was making his way to my door. He opened the door and walked through the passage to the room in which I rested.

As I feared, it was the monster. Once

again, he accused me of destroying his chances of happiness.

"Go away!" I cried.

He threatened to make me even more miserable than I already was, but I held my ground.

"Your threats do not scare me," I said. "They only convince me that I am right to deny your wishes. Be gone. Trouble humanity no more!"

"Beware, for I am fearless and therefore powerful," he answered. "I will watch for opportunities to strike back. Beware!"

"Devil!" I cried.

"I will go," he said. "But I will be with you on your wedding night."

I rushed at him, attempting to seize him. But he ran out of the hut. I heard him climb into his boat and paddle away.

CHAPTER 17

The Monster Strikes Again!

When morning came, I left the hut and walked around the island, wishing that I could pass the rest of my wretched life here. I saw a fishing boat land close to me. One of the men aboard brought me a packet containing letters from Geneva. There was one from Henry requesting that I meet him at Perth so we could travel south together. His request stirred me to action.

Under the cover of night I put my instruments in a basket filled with stones. I boarded a little boat and sailed out about four miles from shore. A few

boats were returning to the island, but no one seemed to notice me. I flung the basket overboard and lay down in the boat to rest. When I woke, the sun had already risen. The wind was strong. I could not navigate my course, and I wasn't familiar enough with the area to know where I was directed.

I spent quite a few hours in fear of being lost, stranded or drowned. But these dark thoughts were relieved when I saw land up ahead. I made a sail with part of my clothing and steered the boat toward the shore. As I got closer, I could make out a small town with a harbor.

A man came close and said, "Come, sir, you must follow me to Mr. Kirwin's to give an account of yourself."

"Who is Mr. Kirwin?" I asked. "Why am I to give an account of myself?"

"Mr. Kirwin is a magistrate," the man said. "You are to give an account of the death of a gentleman who was found murdered here last night."

I stood before the crowd in shock. I had been accused of murder in a strange place, with no friends or family to come to my aid!

Mr. Kirwin was a kind and gentle man. But the look on his face told me that the accusation was serious. One witness came forward to say that he had been out fishing the night before with his son and brother-in-law. At about ten o'clock they felt a strong wind and decided to return to the port. They did not land at the harbor, but at a creek about two miles below. He walked on ahead while his companions followed at some distance. His foot struck against something on the ground, and he fell. When his companions reached him, they helped him up. By the light of their lantern, they saw that the object was the body of a man who, it appeared, was dead. The person had not drowned, for his clothes were dry and the body was not yet cold.

The men had carried the body to the cottage of an old woman close by. When they examined the body, they judged that he had been strangled to death, since there were some black marks on his neck where huge fingers might have choked him. At the mention of the huge fingers, the monster came to my mind. I trembled, and I saw Mr. Kirwin take note of my agitation.

The fisherman's son-in-law then spoke up to say that he had seen a boat near shore, and a single man was on board. Other people came forward

to confirm and add to this testimony. Clearly, these people thought that I had killed the man.

When the testimonies were finally completed, Mr. Kirwin took me into another room to view the body. How can I describe my dismay at seeing before me the cold and stiff body of my beloved friend Henry? Henry, who had been so young and full of life, with a great future before him, was dead! And my monster was to blame! A swirl of confusion swam over me. The next thing I knew, I was in a prison, stretched out on a miserable cot and surrounded by iron bars and guards. For two months I lay raving and feverish, with only Mr. Kirwin to show me some kindness and compassion. He did not visit often, but he made sure that I had the best room in the prison and a nurse to watch over me.

As Mr. Kirwin seemed to know a bit about me, I asked how he had come by this information. He replied that he

had read through all of the papers that had been found in my possession and had contacted my father. Mr. Kirwin assured me that all was well in Geneva. In fact, someone from Geneva was on his way to visit me.

Mr. Kirwin left me for a few moments and returned with my father. We embraced, and he told me that everyone at home was in good health. Then sadness came over his features as he mentioned poor Henry. What could I say? I just stared in anguish at both my father and Mr. Kirwin. Before long, they left me to rest.

My father stayed on until the trial, which took place after I had spent three months in prison. Mr. Kirwin arranged for my defense, and all went smoothly. I was set free, but this gave me no joy. The future looked bleak. I would go back home with my father and marry Elizabeth, but the monster would now stalk us both. Who would be his next victim?

CHAPTER 18

Victor Marries Elizabeth

I was deeply troubled throughout our voyage home. Our first stop was Paris, and my father judged that we should stop here while I gathered my strength. He was alarmed that I kept blaming myself for the deaths of William, Justine, and now Henry. Hoping to keep me calm, he avoided any subject that would lead my thoughts to these misfortunes.

In the middle of May, we decided to start our journey home. A few days before we left Paris for Switzerland, I received a letter from Elizabeth. Her words were comforting, but brought to

139

mind the monster's parting threat. Would he find us on our wedding night? How could I protect my beloved Elizabeth?

Before leaving Paris, I wrote back to her that my heart was set on our union. I vowed to myself that I would not let the monster destroy my beloved. I felt that I must reveal my terrible secret to her, but not until after we were married. I told her this in my letter, but urged her not to think about it until after the wedding.

A week later, I was standing before her, and all thoughts of the monster fled from my mind.

She was thinner and had lost much of her childlike exuberance. Looking at her trusting face, I became more enraged at the monster's wish to destroy our future happiness. When my father urged that we set a date for the wedding, I halfheartedly complied. I felt as though fate were pulling me along, and I did not have the strength to do anything but follow.

After the ceremony, a large party

gathered at our house to celebrate. It was agreed that Elizabeth and I would leave right away to begin our honeymoon journey by sea.

Those were my last moments of happiness. The weather was beautiful, the scenery breathtaking, and I was with my beloved.

It was eight o'clock when we landed at Evian. We walked for a short time on the shore and then retired to the inn. The wind, which had fallen in the south, now rose with great violence in the west. The moon had risen, and clouds swept across it and dimmed its rays. Suddenly a heavy rainstorm broke.

Every sound terrified me, but I was determined to defend my bride at any cost.

Elizabeth asked, "What is it that troubles you, Victor?" I told her that all would be well, but I did not want her to witness the battle I expected. I told her to go to bed and that I would soon join her. After she left, I walked up and down the hallways of the inn and

inspected every corner. There was no trace of the monster. Just when I had decided that perhaps we were safe, I heard Elizabeth scream. I ran to our room. There she lay, lifeless across the bed! I cried out in pain and threw myself down on the floor.

Soon a crowd of people formed outside the room. They were alarmed by the screams that had echoed throughout the inn. I hung over Elizabeth's body. A streak of light from the pale moon came through the open window,

drawing my attention. Looking in was the face of the monster! I rushed toward the window, but he fled.

A group of men went outside to look for the murderer, and I tried to follow. But I was seized by a fit. Some of the men carried me back inside and placed me on a bed. I was hardly conscious of what had happened. My eyes wandered around the room as if to seek something that I had lost. My one clear thought was to return to Geneva.

Delivering the news to my father was the most painful thing I had yet endured. He broke under the strain of losing Elizabeth, whom he considered his only daughter. It was not long before he, too, died.

For months after that, I was confined to a cell and treated as a madman. When I had stopped raving, I was

released. But freedom meant nothing to me now. I sought one thing: revenge!

I told my tale to a magistrate, hoping to get his help to hunt down the demon. The magistrate was kind and patient. He did not question the truth of my story. But he said it would be impossible to capture a man of such strength and endurance. He asked me where the monster now was. When I told him that I did not know, the magistrate said that it was possible that the monster was far from Geneva already, which would make it even more difficult to capture him. I left the magistrate and decided to take justice into my own hands.

CHAPTER 19

Victor Seeks Revenge

Before leaving Geneva, I visited the graves of William, Elizabeth and my father. I vowed to capture the demon who had ruined my life!

A loud and fiendish laugh rang out to answer me.

The monster shouted, "I am satisfied, miserable wretch! You have determined to live, and I am satisfied."

I darted toward the spot from which the sound came. But the monster was gone when I got there. Suddenly the broad disk of the moon arose and shone full upon his ghastly and distorted shape as he fled with more than mortal speed.

I spent many months traveling in pursuit, following clues left behind by the fiend. I saw him board a ship heading for the Black Sea. I, too, boarded the ship, but he had escaped. Sometimes he left clues for me to find. He led me to the most desolate, barren places, far from all traces of civilization. I do not know how I was able survive the hardship, hunger and thirst. I believe that a spirit gave me strength to fulfill my promise to make the demon pay for his crimes.

As I moved northward, the landscape grew more snowy and cold. Everything, it seemed, turned to ice. Some weeks before this period I had hired a sled and dogs, which greatly aided my progress over the snow and ice. I now gained on him, so much so that when I first saw the ocean he was but one day's journey ahead of me.

Two days later I arrived at a hamlet on the seashore. Some of the inhabitants had seen the monster and pointed out

his direction. He had arrived the night before, armed with many pistols. He had carried off their store of winter food. Taking a sled and a team of trained dogs, he continued his journey across the sea in a direction that led to no land. I exchanged my land-sled for one more suited to the frozen ocean and, purchasing a plentiful stock of provisions, I departed from land. I don't know how many days passed since then, but I endured much misery and hardship in my pursuit.

I almost gave in to despair, but then I looked over the sea of ice before me. I saw a dark spark on the horizon. It was a sled! Aboard was a huge figure.

My heart leaped with joy. I must keep going! I urged the team on and followed the speck for nearly two days. I gained on him and soon I was no more than a mile away from him.

But now, when I appeared almost within grasp of my enemy, the ice began to break up. In a few minutes the sea was let loose and swelled between the monster and me. I was left drifting on a piece of ice that continued to break up. Several of my dogs died, and I was about to collapse when I saw your vessel. I was able to construct oars with pieces of the sled, and by this means I moved my ice raft in the direction of your ship.

Swear to me, Walton, that if I die, you will seek him and put an end to his life. When I am dead, if he should appear, swear that he will not be allowed to continue to murder the innocent. He certainly will try to gain your compassion, but do not trust him. He will continue his miserable acts until he is stopped.

CHAPTER 20

Walton Continues the Story

To Mrs. Saville, England
August 26, 17–

Dear Margaret,

Now that you have read this strange and terrifying tale, I have no doubt that you question its truth. I must tell you that I believe the story. His face, his voice, everything about this man spoke of the pain and hardship he endured during these trials. Frankenstein discovered that I made notes concerning his history. He asked to see them and then corrected and added to them in many places. The only thing he would not

relate to me was how he had formed the monster. He told me to learn from his mistakes and not indulge a curiosity that would lead to a similar fate.

Thus a week has passed while I have listened to him tell of his experiences—each one more amazing than the last. I wish to soothe him, yet what can I say to one so miserable? His dreams, he says, are his one consolation. In them, his loved ones visit him and restore in him a measure of peace.

Our conversations are not always so painful. Sometimes he becomes quite animated as we discuss literature and other subjects that are dear to his heart. Before his trials, he must have been a noble being. His intelligence and wisdom have made a strong impression on me.

R.W.

To Mrs. Saville, England
September 2, 17–

My dearest sister,

I am surrounded by mountains of ice and am fearful for our future. It gives me great pain to think of endangering the lives of the men who trust me in this way. If we are lost, my mad schemes are the cause. And what, Margaret, will become of you? I do not want you to wait anxiously for word of our safety, or of our ruin. But you have a husband and lovely children. May you all be happy, come what may!

Frankenstein's presence with us has been a blessing. He reminds me of how often the same accidents have happened to other pioneers. Even the sailors are cheered and reassured by his words of encouragement.

With love,
Robert Walton

To Mrs. Saville, England

September 5, 17–

We are still surrounded by mountains of ice. The cold is unbearable, and many of my unfortunate comrades have died. Frankenstein is ill, and his health declines with each day. I fear that the remaining crew members are planning a mutiny. This morning, a dozen of the sailors barged into the cabin. Their leader told me that he and his companions had been chosen by the other sailors to come and insist that, if by some miracle the ice dissolved and the way made clear for travel, we must change our course and return to the south.

I admit that I did not want to give up yet, even if my men felt that their lives were in danger. I still had my dreams of glory. Yet could I refuse their demand?

As I hesitated, Frankenstein spoke up. "What do you mean? Are you, then, so easily turned from your duty? Did you not call this a glorious expedition? If it be glorious, it will not be because the way was smooth. It will be because you overcame danger and had the courage to persevere through hardship and deprivation. Return as heroes who have fought and conquered."

The men looked at one another and were unable to reply. I told them to consider what had been said. I promised that I would not lead them farther north if they did not want to proceed, but that I hoped their courage would return. After they left

us, I turned toward my friend, but he was so weak, he could no longer speak.

I do not know how this will end, Margaret. I do hope that I will survive long enough to notify you of our decision.

R. W.

To Mrs. Saville, England
September 12, 17–

Beloved sister,

It is settled. We are returning to England. My dream has come to an end, and I have lost my noble friend. I will tell you of his death, dear sister.

On September 9, the ice began to move. The sound of cracking, like thunder, filled the air. The islands of ice began to dissolve in every direction. Although we were in grave danger, my main concern was for Frankenstein. He was very ill and confined to his bed. The ice cracked behind us and was driven with force toward the north. A breeze sprang up from the west, and on the 11th a passage toward the south

became clear. When the sailors saw this, they shouted for joy. Frankenstein, who had been dozing, woke up and asked what had happened.

"They are happy," I said, "because they will soon return to England."

"Then you will return?" he asked, looking disappointed.

"I must," I answered.

"Do so, if you must. But I cannot go with you. I am weak, but surely the spirits who have come to my aid before will help me to accomplish my task." He tried to rise from the bed, but fell back and fainted.

It was a long time until he regained consciousness. He breathed with difficulty and was unable to speak. The surgeon gave him some medicine and asked the others not to disturb him. In private, the surgeon told me that my friend had certainly not many hours to live.

I sat by my friend's bed and watched him. His eyes were closed, and I thought

he was sleeping. After a little while, he called to me in a feeble voice.

"The strength I relied on is gone," he said. "I feel that I will soon die, and my enemy may still be alive. I no longer feel the hatred toward him that I felt these past months, but I feel myself justified in desiring his death. In a fit of madness I gave life to this creature and was then obligated, as far as it was in my power, to attend to his happiness and well-

being. Still, I owed far more to my fellow men. I could not allow this demon to murder more innocent victims. The task of his destruction was mine, but I have failed. I once again ask that you fulfill this task, now that my life is coming to an end."

He hesitated for a moment. When he continued, he said, "But I cannot ask you to forsake your own future. Farewell, Walton! Seek happiness in

peace, and avoid ambition." His voice grew fainter as he spoke, and he sank into silence. About half an hour later he tried to speak but was unable. He pressed my hand feebly, and his eyes closed forever.

Margaret, what can I say to describe this man? What can I say that will help you understand the depth of my sorrow on losing this noble creature? The friend I thought I would never find has come, only to leave so soon.

It is midnight, and I should retire now. But I am interrupted. What do these sounds mean? They come from the cabin where Frankenstein rests, still and cold. I must go see who is disturbing his peace. Good night, my sister.

Yours truly,
Robert Walton

To Mrs. Saville, England
September 13, 17–

Dear Margaret,

If Frankenstein's tale seemed incredible to you, what I am about to write will most certainly shock you. I entered Frankenstein's cabin and saw, towering over him, the monster of which he spoke. Long locks of ragged hair hid his face. When he heard me approaching, he sprang toward the window. I was then able to see fully his hideous face and figure. I closed my eyes, repulsed by this vision of horror. He looked like an animated mummy.

"He is also my victim!" he exclaimed. "Oh, Frankenstein! I now ask you to pardon me, but it is too late to receive your forgiveness."

I approached him but dared not raise my eyes to his face. There was something unearthly about his ugliness. I tried to speak, but choked on the words. Finally, I pulled myself together and *addressed him.*

"Your request for forgiveness is, indeed, too late. Frankenstein is gone, and you are the cause."

"Do you think that he was the only one to suffer?" he asked. "I only wanted friendship. I was good and desired goodness until man turned his back on me and made me an enemy. It was only then that I began my evil ways. You may hate me, but it is nothing compared to the hatred I feel for myself."

I was at first touched by the pain on his face, but I recalled what Frankenstein had said about the monster and how he would try to gain my sympathy. I did not allow myself to be taken in by the monster.

"You are a most wretched creature!" I cried. "If you are in pain, it is certainly not because you feel sorry for your crimes."

"It is true that I am a wretch," he replied. "I have murdered the lovely and

the helpless. I have tormented my creator and caused endless misery. Fear not. My work is nearly complete. One more death is required, and it is my own. Soon Frankenstein's monster will be no more. Farewell."

With that, he sprang from the cabin window. He was soon swept away by the waves into the dark distance never to be seen again.

Here, my dear Margaret, ends the sad story of Victor Frankenstein and his monster.

The End

About the Author

Born in London on August 30, 1797, Mary Wollstonecraft Godwin came from a talented family. Her father was the novelist and political journalist, William Godwin. Her mother, Mary Wollstonecraft, wrote an important book on women's rights, *Vindication of the Rights of Woman.*

Mary was not formally educated, but she read many books and absorbed the literary atmosphere of the household.

In 1816, at the age of 19, Mary wed poet Percy Bysshe Shelley and joined his literary circle. In the summer of 1816, during a stay near Geneva, Switzerland, her husband and his friends challenged her to write a ghost story, and so she began to write what became her most famous work, *Frankenstein.*

After her husband's death in 1822, Shelley wrote four more novels and contributed occasional stories to popular literary journals. She died in 1851.